P9-BYQ-655

No, David!

By

David Shannon

THE BLUE SKY PRESS

An Imprint of Scholastic Inc. • New York

To Martha, my mother, who kept me in line then,

and to Heidi, my wife, who keeps me in line now.

AUTHOR'S NOTE

A few years ago, my mother sent me a book I made when I was a little boy. It was called *No, David*, and it was illustrated with drawings of David doing all sorts of things he wasn't supposed to do. The text consisted entirely of the words "no" and "David." (They were the only words I knew how to spell.) I thought it would be fun to do a remake celebrating those familiar variations of the universal "no" that we all hear while growing up.

Of course, "yes" is a wonderful word. . . but "yes" doesn't keep crayon off the living room wall.

THE BLUE SKY PRESS

Library of Congress catalog card number: 97035125
ISBN-13: 978-0-590-93002-4 / ISBN-10: 0-590-93002-8
60 59 58 57 56 21 22 23 24 25
Printed in China 38
First printing, September 1998

David's mom always said...

No, David!

NO, DAVID!

OOKIES
UGAR
LOUR

No, David, no!

No! No! No!

Come back

here, David!

DAVID!
BE QUIET!

Don't play
with your
food!

That's enough,

David!

Go to

your room!

SETTLE
DOWN!

Stop
that
this
instant!

Put your
toys away!

Not in the

house, David!

I said
no, David!

Davey,

come here.

Yes, David...
I love you!